for Jonathan

All rights reserved. Published by Scholastic Inc.
SCHOLASTIC, CARTWHEEL BOOKS, and associated logos are trademarks and/or registered trademarks of Scholastic Inc.
Library of Congress Cataloging-in-Publication Data is available.

Design by Angela Navarra

ISBN 978-0-545-12104-0

10 9 8 7 6 5 4 3 2 1   10 11 12 13 14

Printed in China 62
First edition, March 2010

ASTROBLAST!
CODE BLUE

BOB KOLAR

Cartwheel
·B·O·O·K·S· ®

Scholastic Inc.
New York   Toronto   London   Auckland
Sydney   Mexico City   New Delhi   Hong Kong

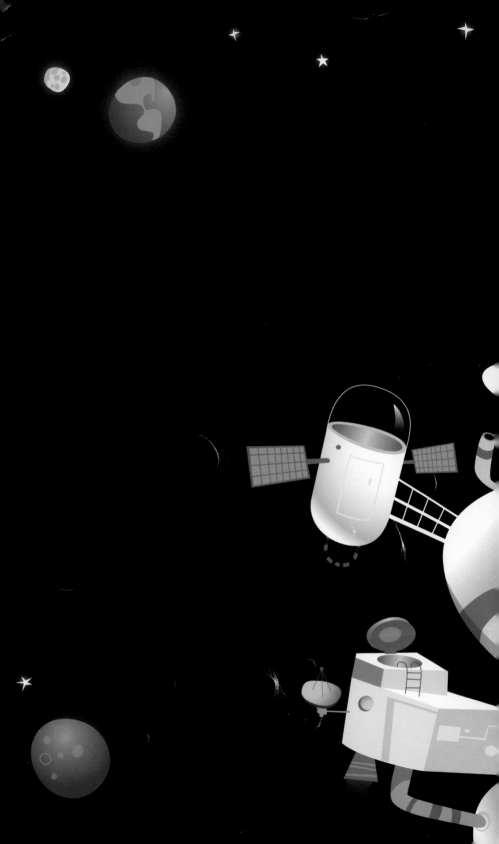

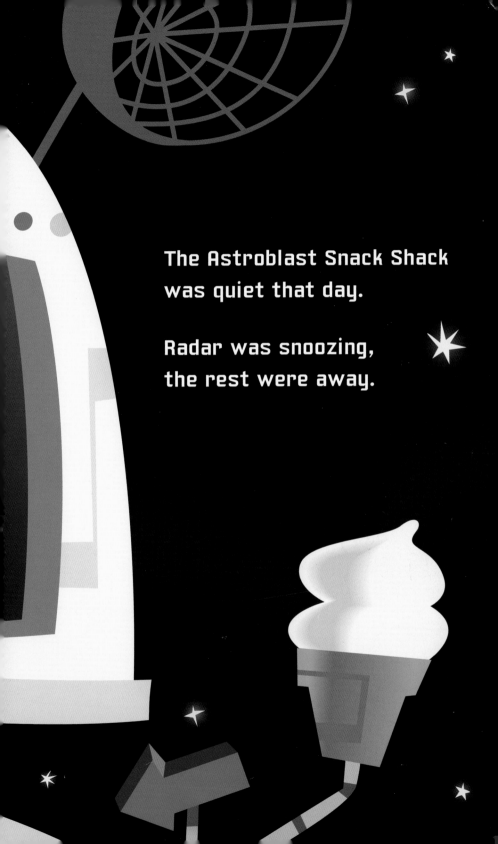

The Astroblast Snack Shack
was quiet that day.

Radar was snoozing,
the rest were away.

An alarm sounded out.
Radar fell on his rear.

"I must tell my friends—
they need to be here."

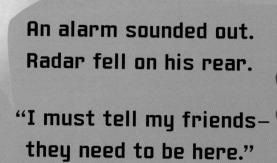

CODE BLUE
CODE BLUE
But where is the crew?

Apollo was fixing some broken-down rockets.

Apollo's tools are floating all over the space dock. Help him find them all.

"Bow wowza!" He jumped, and
spilled hammers and sockets.

Halley was out finding
comets to race.

She shouted out, "Whoa!"
and gave up the chase.

Halley has a long trip back to the Astroblast Snack Shack.

Help her take a shortcut through the asteroid field.

Jet had just dug up
a shiny moon stone.

Jet has dug up too many moon stones. Can you fit each one bac

"Well, jeepers," he thought.
"I must get back home."

nto the right hole?

Sputnik was looking
for junk out in space.

"Not now!" she snorted,
and made a mad face.

Sputnik found two spaceships in the junkyard that are not as simi

s they seem. Can you spot the 7 differences?

"Where is everyone?"
shouted Radar with fear.

"An alarm has gone off.
Did anyone hear?"

CODE BLUE
CODE BLUE
There's so much to do!

The countdown has begun. Help Radar find these hidden numbers.

Apollo and Halley
came back in a rush.

Then Sputnik and Jet,
in a cloud of moondust.

Which of the 4 buttons should Radar push to open the right hatch?

CODE BLUE
CODE BLUE
They knew what to do.

The Astroblast Snack Shack is a wacky place, but not *this* wacky.

Can you find 5 things that are wrong with this picture?

The crew forgot to make a sign for the party.

They made Glob Cluster Candies
and Milky Way Shakes.

They made Gamma Ray Pizzas
and Creamy Moon Cakes.

Find the hidden letters they need to spell **W E L C O M E**.

They treated their friends
to a wonderful snack.

An Astroblast welcome
for guests to the shack.

A is for Aliens and Astroblast.

Can you find at least 5 other things that begin with **A**?

"I'm tired," said Radar.
"Can I go to bed?"

Then a new sound was heard....

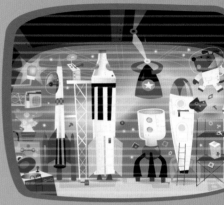
Activity 1

Activity 4

Activity 7

ANSWER KEY

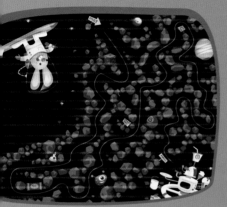

Activity 2

Activity 3

Activity 5

Activity 6

Activity 8

Activity 9

EXTRA MISSIONS

1 We have 8 planets in our solar system, 9 if you count Pluto. Can you spot them in this book?

Mercury · Earth · Venus · Mars · Jupiter · Saturn · Uranus · Neptune · Pluto

2 Sputnik is a DJ, but she has trouble keeping track of her record collection. Help her find the 4 that are missing.

3 Oops, Apollo knocked over his toolbox again! Can you find the tools on the other pages?

4 It's break time at the Snack Shack, and Halley wants to play a game. Can you find:

a baseball

a tennis racket

an eight ball

a pair of dice

a soccer ball

a bowling pin

There have been blue aliens and a red alien, but can you find a green alien?

Jet packed a tasty lunch in his backpack, but it all fell out. Can you find the 8 slices of his Gamma Ray Pizza?

Everyone dropped something important when they heard the CODE BLUE. Can you find:

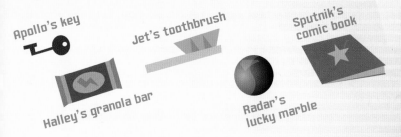

Apollo's key

Jet's toothbrush

Sputnik's comic book

Halley's granola bar

Radar's lucky marble

Radar wanted to go out on a spacewalk, but he couldn't find his jet pack, gloves, helmet, and boots. Can you?

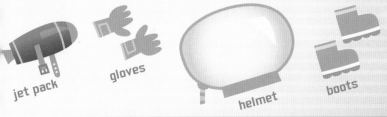

jet pack

gloves

helmet

boots

Did you find 5 things that began with the letter "A" on the party page? Good job—now try to find 5 more!

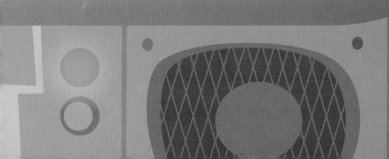